Folk Tales o

How the Red Ants
Got Their Color

By I. Carole Husbands

Folk Tales of the Caribbean: How the Red Ants got their Color Copyright © 2020 by I. Carole Husbands All rights reserved. This book or any portion thereof may not be reproduced or used in any manner whatsoever without the express written permission of the publisher except for the use of brief quotations in a book review.

Printed in the United States of America

First Printing, November 2020

ISBN 9798696229454

For

David and Chantal Marley Husbands

Shawn Jr., Shareka, Shanell and Shamoi Ferris

Ashan, Shana and Ashna Austin

Jessica and Jazmine Grell

Alden Pole, Russell Robinson, Rhudell Huyghue

Children of E. Benjamin Oliver Elementary School,
St. Thomas U.S. Virgin Islands

I am sitting at my desk, staring out of the window, on the fifteenth floor, instead of finishing up my project. It is a perfect day. I can see people perched on benches and a few sitting on well placed napkins, in the green space area eating lunch. Several little children are splashing around in the reflecting pond as Security guards stroll along the sidewalk. It is really time for a break, I said to myself. I looked around the office only to see my coworkers faces buried in their computers or notebooks. That settles it; I say as I push away from my desk, I need some lunch. I turned off my computer and made my way to the hallway toward the exit. There was a bit of a crowd at the elevator, so I took the stairs to the fourteenth floor and got on the elevator there. It was beautiful outside. The air was humid, but that was a usual summer day in Atlanta. After finding an empty bench, I unwrapped my turkey and cheese sandwich, but instantly lost my taste for food. I was more interested in the kids playing in the water, than I was in my sandwich. I got so lost in thought that I did not notice that a little red ant had climbed across my sandwich, and bit my finger. I shook it off and watched as it crawled across the bench and disappeared into the grass. Although the ant bite stung, I found myself laughing out loud. This moment triggered a memory from my childhood in the Caribbean.

I was about five years old, living on the island of Saint Thomas, in an area called Bordeaux. It was green and pretty, with lots of flowering trees and nice neighbors. I usually spent most of my day at school learning about letters and colors, but on weekends I got

to go to the beach or play with my friends. School was great, and I had lots of fun there, but the best part of school happened at two-thirty, because that was when the bell rang. It was time to go home. The most favorite thing about going home was seeing my Great Aunt Tina. She would meet my school bus at the bottom of the hill, and we would both walk up together. We would wave at all of the neighbors as we passed by. They would wave back and yell out "Hey Miss Tina, everything good with you"? She would reply and continue to walk up the hill. I loved to watch my Aunts' long white braids bop up and down as she moved along. I knew she would have a cinnamon sweet potato muffin and a cold juice box for me when we got to the house. How did I know? Because that is what she did every day. I could not wait to get through with my homework so that she could tell me a story. It was our best time together. Aunt Tina would sit in her big chair, with me on her lap, and the cool breeze blowing across the porch. I would eat my muffin, drink my juice box and listen to her stories. It was the best time ever.

"Tally", Aunt Tina would call out to me. I would have already finished up my homework; changed out of my school uniform and put on my play clothes. I was always ready for a story.

"Coming Aunt Tina", I would shout from the back bedroom, "I'm coming as fast as I can". I would make my way to the front porch to sit with her. This was our routine every day that I had school. My weekends were spent mostly with my Mom and older brother, running errands, shopping and of course church on Sunday. Dad was always working on an old blue Chevy that was in the back yard, resting on two cement blocks. He had been working on that car for as longs as I can remember.

This particular day after Aunt Tina called me to join her on the front porch. I stopped in the doorway to watch two birds picking at a mango that sat high on the tree.

"Those old birds are going to get all the good mangoes", Aunt Tina had said as she motioned to them. She was trying to shoo them, but she was too far away. "Birds always know when the mangoes are ripe and these two just happened to be picking at the one, I had my eye on". We had both giggled at the thought of my Aunt Tina climbing way up into her mango tree to pick that fruit. "Come on now and get cozy", she had told me, as she went back to her big chair, with me happily following behind her.

"Can you tell me about the Ants"?, I had asked. "You said you would tell me the story about the ants the next time we were together, so this has got to be the day". I had given her my big, hopeful eyes, batted my lashes and smiled.

"All right, you got it", Aunt Tina had smiled. She nestled me in her bosom, got comfortable and spoke to me in her warm and comforting voice.

"Hey, you kids", a man was shouting.

I snapped out of my daydream as I heard two security guards talking to the children that were playing in the reflecting pond. They were asked to point out their parents, because the reflecting pond was for admiring, and not swimming or splashing in. When no parents were to be found, the guards were telling the children that they were not allowed on the property without adult supervision. The tall security guard was about to ask the children to leave the property when I called out to the kids.

"Excuse me", I stood up and faced the guards, "do you kids want to hear a story until your parents come back"? Their faces lit up as they ran over to me. The security guards being satisfied that the children were no longer unattended, both walked away having accomplished some order to the area for the time being. With seven little children sitting at my feet, I asked them the same questions my Aunt Tina asked me years ago.

"Do you all know why red ants are red"?

"They just are", a little girl with lopsided pigtails, said to me. She was sitting in the grass with her legs crossed and her elbows resting on her knees; looking up at me matter of factually.

"Oh really", I replied. "What if I tell you I know the real story about why red ants are actually red, and not black or brown"? All of the children were silent as I continued.

"I'm going to tell you a story my Aunt Tina told me when I was a little girl", I said as I leaned in to them, and began my tale.

A long, long time ago; way, way back when they didn't have fast cars and jumbo airplanes, they had slow busses, little corner grocery stands and iron roller skates. Everybody on the Caribbean island of Saint Thomas, who lived in an area called Bordeaux, kept busy by crafting things to sell and wear or work the land. Calvin Petersen lived there with his wife Naomi. They had three acres of the most beautiful land you ever wanted to see. They had chickens that gave them eggs, so Naomi could bake and sell her goods, but their life was spent working the land. They were yam farmers. Well, what you call sweet potatoes here in Atlanta, they called them yams in Saint Thomas. So let me get back to the story. The Petersen's did not do all of the farming alone, they had the assistance of their four children.

Calvin was the proud father of three boys. The older people often said that boy children bring wealth and prosperity to the household. He loved his three sons, but they were very lazy and so far, brought no great riches to the family, only grocery debt. Treshawn, the oldest, often fell asleep while tending to the repairs of the property. Uriah, the middle son, would wander off for long periods of time instead of watering the yams; and JoJo, the youngest son, was too small to do anything except to assist his mother with weed pulling and little house chores. Calvin's pride and joy came to him in the form of his only daughter, Adriane. She was a hard worker and adored her father. She was the only one who would get out into the field with him to harvest yams. It was tedious work that required a great deal of bending and toting. Adriane was also the only one who would go on long walks with her father and learn about planting techniques and soil condition; and it was Adriane that brought him his dinner and sat with him on the front porch while he listed to the baseball games on the radio. One summer, the Petersen household had an abundant harvest and the money they made selling their yams was more than enough to take care of the family expenses. To show his appreciation for all of Adriane's hard work, he decided to take her on an outing.

Naomi packed a great feast for her husband and daughter. She made sure that their water jugs were filled with cold spring water and that their back packs were full of delicious food. She even packed her husband his favorite desert, cinnamon sweet potato

muffins. Naomi had learned to make the muffins from her mother, my Great Aunt Tina. Treshawn and Uriah begged to go along, but Calvin told them that they had to stay behind and assist their mother with the planting of the new yams. They also had to keep an eye out for their little brother JoJo.

Calvin and Adriane started off on their trip. They got on the Bordeaux bus and headed to town. The bus passed by Santa Maria beach with its rock doted shoreline; then headed toward Estate Pearl. It moved down the hill and I got a glimpse of the Adams' property, which was one of the prettiest homes on the north side. The large white house rested high on the hill, with several wrap around porches on each level. The stone fence was close to the main road and was lined with flamboyant trees that were always in full bloom. The large pumpkin colored blossoms were nestled on finger like branches, draped with an overcoat of green leaves. Down the hills and around the winding turns were brightly colored homes, lush foliage and an array of flowering shrubs. There were also bursts of blue and snatches of the turquoise ocean that flew by the window. The bus traveled passed the University of the Virgin Islands that had hundreds of Pindo palm trees. The bus continued along from out of the hills and was now riding along the downtown

streets. All of the passengers got off of the bus by the Waterfront's fruit and fish stand, and the bus continued on its way to the depot. Adriane and her dad walked along the waterfront, through Hibiscus Alley, then toward the ninety-nine steps. There were really over one hundred steps, but it has been called ninety-nine steps for so long, that I don't think anybody ever thought to change the name. Adriane and Calvin took their time walking up each step. They were going higher and higher with each step. She looked down the stairs at the bustling capital city of Charlotte Amalie beneath her. Off in the distance, she could see the cruise ships docked in the harbor, red roofs of the houses along the main street and saw Fort Christian which was the old police station. She stood there for a while, enjoying the sights and catching her breath.

"Let's go slow poke", her father shouted, "I'm hungry". They walked around for a bit, then finally settled on a cool spot at the base of the great Tamarind tree. People say that the tree is over 100 years old.

"Daddy", Adriane started, "do you think we will have time to walk around town before the sun goes down"? She was laying out the blanket for the food, careful to get rid of small rocks and all the creases. The old people in Bordeaux always said that creases in your blanket bring ants, and she did not want any

stupid ants spoiling her perfect day.

"It all depends on how long it takes us to finish all of this food", her father answered. The two travelers sat down on the blanket to eat. The blanket was beautiful. It was filled with large, green ivy leaves, as well as dark pink and bright green hibiscus embroidered around the edges. There were also white tasseled fringes around each of its corners. The blanket was handed down for three generations of the Petersen family, and Adriane could not wait until one day it would be passed down to her. They began to feast upon fried plantains, tuna fish sandwiches, sliced avocado, mango, stewed cherries and cinnamon sweet potato muffins for dessert.

"That all sounds yummy", one of the boys said as he rubbed his tummy. "I wish I had a cinnamon sweet potato muffin right about now".

"Yes" and "Me too", said the other children. "What happens next", they asked.

Well our two travelers continued their lunch. The spring water was cold, and it felt good going down

Adriane's throat. The sun was still high, causing beads of sweat to form on her brow. Calvin was reaching for some sliced avocado when he noticed an army of black ants marching across the left corner of the blanket.

"What is this", he cried out, "black ants on MY blanket". He jumped to his feet and darted toward the end of the blanket. "You didn't get all of the creases out after you laid it down Adriane", he exclaimed, "look at all those crumples in the corner".

"But Daddy", she said in a low tone, "I thought I got all the creases out and made sure there were no small rocks or ant holes on the spot we chose". She quickly began to rearrange the food so that the few brave ants that reached her end of the blanket would not have a chance to carry away the smallest crumb.

Adriane and Calvin began to stomp on the black ants that were around the edges of the blanket. When all of the ants were gone, the blanket and the food were moved to another spot. They were careful not to let any food or crumbs fall from the blanket. They both sat down again and began to enjoy their feast. The sun

was starting to sit just above the roof of the old Grand Hotel, as the cool breeze began to blow off the sea. Calvin was eating some stewed cherries, while Adriane was licking the icing from her fingers, having just eaten one of the cinnamon sweet potato muffins. It was then that Calvin noticed, from the corner of his eye, a small band of black ants charging toward the last muffin.

"What is this", he yelled, "more ants"! He rubbed his eyes in disbelief. "Well, I will put a stop to this right now". He reached into the backpack that contained the rest of the food and pulled out a bottle of red pepper sauce. He poured some of the sauce all over the ants, and more down the ant hole. The little black ants wiggled in the sauce and stumbled back to their holes, only to find that it too was covered in sticky sauce.

"Daddy!" Adriane cried, "the black ants are dragging away your cinnamon sweet potato muffin". She sat up on her knees to watch as the tiny ants pulled the large muffin toward their hole. There must have been hundreds of black ants carrying that muffin, but how were they going to get such a big muffin into their hole? Adriane watched as the ants took that muffin apart, and carried it crumb-by-crumb right into their hole.

"I have had enough", Calvin yelled, "These black ants will never bother anyone else again". He picked up

the red pepper sauce and crawled on all fours to the other ant hole that he found. Calvin poured the entire bottle down the hole and put his hand over it, so that no ants could escape. He laughed to himself, proud of what he had just accomplished. The laughter soon turned to shrieks of pain in a matter of seconds.

"YEEEOOOOWWWW!", bellowed Calvin as he jumped to his feet. He was shaking the hand that he had just covered the ant hole with. "Those ants bit me", he hollered in disbelief, "and it hurts". Adriane grabbed her water jug and poured some cold water over her dads' hand. The water was soothing and made him feel better instantly. Calvin was so busy taking care of his hand that he did not notice that hundreds of red ants began to emerge from the hole. They were upset that Calvin had covered them with such a sticky sauce, and turned their beautiful black skin to red. The ants were so angry that they began to bite Calvin's toes. Then they marched over to Adriane and started to sting her ankles and feet.

"Ouch, ouch, ouch!", Adriane yelled as she hopped on one foot. She was running from the ants when she noticed that they had totally covered the blanket and were biting her father's feet.

I stopped the story at that point and noticed that my lunch break was over. I explained to the children that I really had to leave, because my time was up, and I had to return to my desk. The sad faces and disappointed looks got the best of me. They began to plead and beg me to finish the story.

"Just five more minutes, Miss", the little girl with the lopsided pigtails, insisted. I looked up at my building with all the shiny glass windows, then down at the children's eager faces, and decided at that moment that I had to continue the story.

"All right you guys", I smiled, as I was enjoying telling the story as much as they were enjoying listening to it. "Five more minutes", I thought for a moment and said, "Where were we again"?

"The ants were biting Calvin's toes", shouted the boys in the group".

"Oh yes, I do believe that is where I left off". I continued.

"Quick", Calvin told his daughter, "Grab the blanket and let's head back to the north side". Calvin grabbed the water jugs as Adriane stared at the blanket. There were hundreds of thousands of red ants rampaging across the blanket. They completely covered the food and were carrying things back to their hole. How in the world was she supposed to get them off of the blanket without getting bit?

"Oh Daddy", Adriane said with a high pitch in her voice, "how do you suppose I take the blanket away from those ants"? Her father stopped what he was doing and looked at the blanket. "They got very mad at you when you stopped them from getting your cinnamon sweet potato muffin, and they got even more upset when you poured the red pepper sauce on them", she continued. "How do you think they will react when I take the blanket from them"?

Calvin thought for a moment. He grabbed the two jugs and shook them. They still contained water.

"When I count to three", Calvin started, "I will pour the water all over the blanket, you pull your end off of the ground, I will pull the other end and then we will both shake the remaining ants off of it. He opened the jugs and got prepared for action. "Ready", he asked his daughter, "Let's go". Calvin positioned himself and

Adriane got ready.

"One, two, three!", shouted Calvin as he poured the water from both jugs all over the blanket. And that did the trick. Ants scattered everywhere. Calvin and his daughter shook the blanket every way possible until every visible ant was gone.

"Wrap the blanket and jugs up and let's head for the bus stop", he instructed his daughter. Adriane grabbed up their belongings and headed down the hill. They took the ninety-nine steps two at a time and raced to catch the five-thirty bus back to Bordeaux. They made it down the hill just in time for the bus. It was very crowded with people leaving town having just finished a long day at work. Adriane was lucky enough to get a window seat to watch the busy town of Charlotte Amalie fade in the distance. They passed the Adams property just as the sun melted into the sky. The orange hues of the flamboyant trees seemed to blend into the sunset, while the patches of blue water faded into the shades of darkness. They got off the bus in silence and walked down the long road that lead to their home.

"I cannot believe those ants", Calvin said to his daughter, "not only did they change their color, they got so angry that they bit my toes and ate my cinnamon sweet potato muffin". Calvin and Adriane reached their home just as the crescent moon was visible in the sky. Calvin told his wife about the visitors they had during their lunch.

She looked at him strangely, then said,

"Calvin, do you really expect me to believe that tall tale. Everybody knows there are no such things as red ants, only black and brown". She went about her business of cleaning up the dinner dishes. Next Calvin told his sons, about how the ants had attacked their sister and ate his cinnamon sweet potato muffin. All three boys laughed as they rolled along the floor.

"Come on Dad", Uriah said, "red ants"? Calvin felt bad that nobody believed his story, but he knew that it happened. He knew that his daughter saw the entire thing, and that he was telling the truth.

In the morning as the sun rose, Calvin told the story of the ants to every neighbor that passed his gate.

It was the only story that the neighbors were buzzing about for the rest of the afternoon. It was hard to believe, but then again, everybody knows that red pepper sauce can make your tongue dance, so why not black ants?

Naomi had made avocado sandwiches for lunch and was putting the freshly washed clothes in a basket in order to hang them on the line. She spied her grandmothers' blanket at the bottom of the basket and smiled. It brought warm memories to her mind of her Grandmother braiding her hair, while sitting on that very blanket. She shook it out, and then grabbed a few clothespins out of her apron, in preparation to hang it on the clothesline. The breeze was perfect for drying. She hung the blanket, dropped the extra clothespins into her apron and noticed a few red ants scurrying between the grooves of the basket. They were headed to the tall grass.

"What do you know", Naomi said aloud, "red ants". She picked up her basket and returned to her family.

Calvin continued to tell his story of the red ants when he took yams to sell at the Market Square. By the time that Christmas rolled around, red ants began to pop up around the island. The story had reached the east end, and traveled across the harbor to Water Island. It was not long before the story, as well as the red

ants, began to travel throughout the Caribbean.

"WOW", said the little girl with the lopsided pig tails, "is that really where red ants come from?, I see them all the time in my back yard".

"I honestly don't know", I told her, "but I would love to think so". I got up from my bench and picked up my lunch sack. "I really have to go back to work now kids. I hope to see you around sometime".

"We will be sitting her until Ms. Gentry comes down stairs at five o'clock", reported the young man with the sandy hair wearing a grey sweat suit. I waved goodbye and then went back to my desk. After finishing my project, I took the time to type up a little something for each of the kids and put it inside of manila envelopes. I hurried down to the third floor in hopes of catching Ms. Gentry before she left her desk, but I missed her. I managed to catch up to her as she and the kids were leaving the green area.

"Hello Ms. Gentry", I said as I extended my hand filled with envelopes. "I had the pleasure of meeting these kids during my lunch hour and have something for them. Ms. Gentry handed each child an envelope and thanked me. The little girl with the lopsided pigtails opened her envelope right away and pulled out the sheet of paper that was inside. She looked back at me with a big smile on her face and waved. I had enclosed the recipe for cinnamon sweet potato muffins for each child to make at home.

I am so happy right now, that I would like to share the recipe with you as well. It is on the next page.

Enjoy!

Cinnamon Sweet Potato Muffins

Ingredients:

- 2 cups self-rising flour
- 1 cup sugar
- 1 cup brown sugar
- 2 teaspoons ground cinnamon
- 1 teaspoon nutmeg
- 1 egg
- 2 cups cold mashed sweet potatoes (you may substitute with canned yams)
- 1 cup oil (vegetable or canola)

GLAZE:

- 1 cup confectioners' sugar
- 2 tablespoons plus 1-1/2 teaspoons 2% milk
- 1-1/2 teaspoons butter, melted
- 1 teaspoon vanilla extract
- 1/2 teaspoon ground cinnamon

Directions

- Preheat oven to 375°.

- In a large bowl, combine flour, sugar and cinnamon. In a medium bowl, whisk egg, sweet potatoes and oil. Add all of the ingredients of the medium bowl, into the large bowl and stir.

- You can use cup cake liner paper or grease the muffin pan/cups two-thirds full. (I usually use a 1/3 measuring cup, which is perfect for this). Bake 15-18 minutes or until a toothpick inserted in muffin comes out clean. Cool 5 minutes before removing from pans to wire racks.

- In a small bowl, combine glaze ingredients; drizzle over warm muffins.

Note

If you do not have self-rising flour, replace it with all-purpose flour and add for 2 ½ teaspoons of baking powder and 1-teaspoon salt.

Made in United States
Orlando, FL
15 July 2024